Prais

'My suspicion is that when the dust has settled and when the chronicle of twentieth-century American literature comes to be written, history will place Highsmith at the top of the pyramid' A. N. WILSON, *DAILY TELEGRAPH*

'A writer who has created a world of her own – a world claustrophobic and irrational which we enter each time with a sense of personal danger ... Miss Highsmith is the poet of apprehension' GRAHAM GREENE

'Highsmith is a giant of the genre. The original, the best, the gloriously twisted Queen of Suspense' MARK BILLINGHAM

'One thinks of comparing Miss Highsmith only with herself; by any other standard of comparison, one must simply cheer' AUBERON WAUGH

'Highsmith was every bit as deviant and quirky as her mischievous heroes, and didn't seem to mind if everyone knew it' J. G. BALLARD, *DAILY TELEGRAPH*

'One of the greatest modernist writers' GORE VIDAL

'One closes most of her books with a feeling that the world is more dangerous than one had ever imagined' JULIAN SYMONS, *NEW YORK TIMES BOOK REVIEW*

'For eliciting the menace that lurks in familiar surroundings, there's no one like Patricia Highsmith' *TIME*

'No one has created psychological suspense more densely and deliciously satisfying' *VOGUE*

VIRAGO
MODERN CLASSICS

© Ruth Bernhard

Patricia Highsmith (1921–1995) was born in Fort Worth, Texas, and moved to New York when she was six, where she attended the Julia Richman High School and Barnard College. In her senior year she edited the college magazine, having decided at the age of sixteen to become a writer. Her first novel, *Strangers on a Train*, was made into a classic film by Alfred Hitchcock in 1951. *The Talented Mr Ripley*, published in 1955, introduced the fascinating anti-hero Tom Ripley, and was made into an Oscar-winning film in 1999 by Anthony Minghella. Graham Greene called Patricia Highsmith 'the poet of apprehension', saying that she 'created a world of her own – a world claustrophobic and irrational which we enter each time with a sense of personal danger' and *The Times* named her no.1 in their list of the greatest ever crime writers. Patricia Highsmith died in Locarno, Switzerland, in February 1995. Her last novel, *Small g: A Summer Idyll*, was published posthumously the same year.

Sour Tales for Sweethearts

Patricia Highsmith

virago

VIRAGO

This collection first published in Great Britain in 2015 by Virago Press

1 3 5 7 9 10 8 6 4 2

The stories contained in this volume are extracted
from the collection *Little Tales of Misogyny*,
first published by William Heinemann in London 1977

A CIP catalogue record for this book
is available from the British Library.

ISBN 978-0-349-00691-8

Typeset in Goudy by M Rules
Printed and bound in Great Britain by
Clays Ltd, St Ives plc

Papers used by Virago are from well-managed forests
and other responsible sources.

MIX
Paper from
responsible sources
FSC® C104740

Virago Press
An imprint of
Little, Brown Book Group
100 Victoria Embankment
London EC4Y 0DY

An Hachette UK Company
www.hachette.co.uk

www.virago.co.uk

Contents

The Hand

A young man asked a father for his daughter's hand, and received it in a box – her left hand.

Father: 'You asked for her hand and you have it. But it is my opinion that you wanted other things and took them.'

Young man: 'Whatever do you mean?'

Father: 'Whatever do you think I mean? You cannot deny that I am more honourable than you, because you took something from my family without asking, whereas when you asked for my daughter's hand, I gave it.'

Actually, the young man had not done anything

dishonourable. The father was merely suspicious and had a dirty mind. The father could legally make the young man responsible for his daughter's upkeep and soak him financially. The young man could not deny that he had the daughter's hand – even though in desperation he had now buried it, after kissing it. But it was becoming two weeks old.

The young man wanted to see the daughter, and made an effort, but was quite blocked by besieging tradesmen. The daughter was signing cheques with her right hand. Far from bleeding to death, she was going ahead at full speed.

The young man announced in newspapers that she had quit his bed and board. But he had to prove that she had ever enjoyed them. It was not yet 'a marriage' on paper, or in the church. Yet there was no doubt that he had her hand, and had signed a receipt for it when the package had been delivered.

'Her hand in *what*?' the young man demanded of the police, in despair and down to his last penny. 'Her hand is buried in my garden.'

'You are a criminal to boot? Not merely disorganized in your way of life, but a psychopath? Did you by chance cut off your wife's hand?'

'I did not, and she is not even my wife!'

'He has her hand, and yet she is not his wife!' scoffed the men of the law. 'What shall we do with him? He is unreasonable, maybe even insane.'

'Lock him up in an asylum. He is also broke, so it will have to be a State Institution.'

So the young man was locked up, and once a month the girl whose hand he had received came to look at him through the wire barrier, like a dutiful wife. And like most wives, she had nothing to say. But she smiled prettily. His job provided a small pension now, which she was getting. Her stump was concealed in a muff.

Because the young man became too disgusted with her to look at her, he was placed in a more disagreeable ward, deprived of books and company, and he went really insane.

When he became insane, all that had happened to him, the asking for and receiving his beloved's hand, became intelligible to him. He realized what a horrible mistake, crime even, he had been guilty of in demanding such a barbaric thing as a girl's hand.

He spoke to his captors, saying that now he understood his mistake.

'What mistake? To ask for a girl's hand? So did I, when I married.'

The young man, feeling now he was insane beyond repair, since he could make contact with nothing, refused to eat for many days, and at last lay on his bed with his face to the wall, and died.

The Invalid, or, The Bed-Ridden

She had suffered a fall while on a skiing holiday at Chamonix with her boy friend some ten years ago. The injury had something to do with her back. The doctors couldn't find anything, nobody could see anything wrong with her back, but still it hurt, she said. Actually, she was not sure she would get her man unless she pretended an injury, and one acquired when she had been with him. Philippe, however, was quite in love with her, and she need not have worried so much. Still, hooking Philippe very firmly, plus ensuring a life of leisure – not to say flat on her back in bed, or however she chose to lie comfortably, for the rest of her life – was no small gain. It was a big one. How many other women could capture a man for life, give him nothing at all, not even bother to cook his meals, and still be supported in rather fine style?

Some days she got up, mainly out of boredom. She was sometimes up when the sun was shining, but not always. When the sun was not shining, or when there was a threat of rain, Christine felt terrible and kept to her bed. Then her husband Philippe had to go downstairs with the shopping net and come back and cook. All Christine talked about was 'how I feel'. Visitors and friends were treated to a long account of injections, pills, pains in the back which had kept her from sleeping last Wednesday night, and the possibility of rain tomorrow, because of the way she felt.

But she was always feeling rather well when August came, because she and Philippe went to Cannes then. Things might be bad at the very start of August, however, causing Philippe to engage an ambulance to Orly, then a special accommodation on an aeroplane to Nice. In

Cannes she found herself able to go to the beach every morning at 11 a.m., swimming for a few minutes with the aid of water-wings, and to eat a good lunch. But at the end of August, back in Paris, she suffered a relapse from all the excitement, rich food, and general physical strain, and once more had to take to bed, her tan included. She would sometimes expose tanned legs for visitors, sigh with memories of Cannes, then cover up again with sheets and blanket. September heralded, indeed, the onset of grim winter. Philippe couldn't sleep with her now – though for God's sake he felt he had earned better treatment, having worked his fingers to the bone to pay her doctors', radiologists' and pharmacies' bills beyond reckoning. He would have to face another solitary winter, and not even in the same room with her but in the next room.

'To think I brought all this upon her,' Philippe said to one of his friends, 'by taking her to Chamonix.'

'But why is she always feeling quite well in August?' replied the friend. 'You think she is an invalid? Think again, really, old man.'

Philippe did begin to think, because other friends had said the same thing. It took him years to think, many years of Augusts in Cannes (at an expense which knocked out the savings of a whole eleven months) and many winters sleeping mainly in the 'spare bedroom', and not with the woman he loved and desired.

So the eleventh August in Cannes, Philippe summoned all his courage. He swam out behind Christine with a pin in his fingers. He stuck a pin in her water wings and made two punctures, one in each white wing. He and Christine were not far out, just slightly over their heads in water. Philippe was not in the best of form. Not only was he losing his hair, of no importance in a swimming situation, but he had developed a belly, which might not, he thought, have come if he had been able to make love to Christine all the past decade. But Philippe tried and succeeded in pushing Christine under, and at the same time had some difficulty in keeping himself afloat. His confused motions, seen by a few people finally, appeared to be those of a man trying to save someone who was drowning. And this of course was what he told the police and everyone. Christine, despite sufficient buoyant fat, sank like a piece of lead.

Christine was absolutely no loss to Philippe except for burial fees. He soon lost his paunch, and much to his own surprise found himself suddenly well-to-do, instead of having to turn every penny. His friends congratulated him, but politely, and in the abstract. They couldn't exactly say, 'Thank God, you're rid of that bitch,' but they said the next thing to it. In about six months, he met quite a nice girl who loved to cook, was full of energy, and she also liked to go to bed with him. The hair on Philippe's head even began to grow back.

The Fully-Licensed Whore, or, The Wife

Sarah had always played the field as an amateur, and at twenty she got married, which made her licensed. To top it, the marriage was in a church in full view of family, friends and neighbours, maybe even God as witness, for certainly He was invited. She was all in white, though hardly a virgin, being two months pregnant and not by the man she was marrying, whose name was Sylvester. Now she could become a professional, with protection of the law, approval of society, blessing of the clergy, and financial support guaranteed by her husband.

Sarah lost no time. It was first the gas meter reader, to limber herself up, then the window-cleaner, whose job took a varying number of hours, depending on how dirty she told Sylvester the windows had been. Sylvester sometimes had to pay for eight hours' work plus a bit of overtime. Sometimes the window-cleaner was there when Sylvester left for work, and still there when he came home in the evening. But these were small fry, and Sarah progressed to their lawyer, which had the advantage of 'no fee' for any services performed for the Sylvester Dillon family, now three.

Sylvester was proud of baby son Edmund, and flushed with pleasure at what friends said about Edmund's resemblance to himself. The friends were not lying, only saying what they thought they should say, and what they would have said to any father. After Edmund's birth, Sarah ceased sexual relations with Sylvester (not that they'd ever had much) saying, 'One's enough, don't you think?' She could also say, 'I'm tired,' or 'It's too hot.' In plain fact, poor Sylvester was good only for his money – he wasn't wealthy but quite comfortably off – and because he was reasonably intelligent and presentable, not aggressive enough to be a nuisance and – Well, that was about all it took to satisfy Sarah. She had a vague idea that she needed a protector and escort. It somehow carried more weight to write 'Mrs' at the foot of letters.

She enjoyed three or four years of twiddling about with the lawyer, then their doctor, then a couple of maverick husbands in their social circle, plus a few two-week sprees with the father of Edmund. These men visited the house mainly during the afternoons Monday to Friday. Sarah was most cautious and insisted – her house front being visible to several neighbours – that her lovers ring her when they were already in the vicinity, so she could tell them if the coast was clear enough for them to nip in. One-thirty p.m. was the safest time, when most people were eating lunch. After all, Sarah's bed and board was at stake, and Sylvester was becoming restless, though as yet not at all suspicious.

Sylvester in the fourth year of marriage made a slight fuss. His own advances to his secretary and also to the girl who worked behind the counter in his office-supplies shop had been gently but firmly rejected, and his ego was at a low ebb.

'Can't we try again?' was Sylvester's theme.

Sarah counter-attacked like a dozen battalions whose guns had been primed for years to fire. One would have thought she was the one to whom injustice had been done. 'Haven't I created a lovely home for you? Aren't I a good hostess – the *best* according to all our friends, isn't that true? Have I ever neglected Edmund? Have I ever failed to have a hot meal waiting for you when you come home?'

I wish you would forget the hot meal now and then and think of something else, Sylvester wanted to say, but was too well brought up to get the words out.

'Furthermore I have taste,' Sarah added as a final volley. 'Our furniture is not only good, it's well cared for. I don't know what more you can expect from me.'

The furniture was so well polished, the house looked like a museum. Sylvester was often shy about dirtying ashtrays. He would have liked more disorder and a little more warmth. How could he say this?

'Now come and eat something,' Sarah said more sweetly, extending a hand in a burst of contact unprecedented for Sylvester in the past many years. A thought had just crossed her mind, a plan.

Sylvester took her hand gladly, and smiled. He ate second helpings of everything that she pressed upon him. The dinner was as usual good, because Sarah was an excellent and meticulous cook. Sylvester was hoping for a happy end to the evening also, but in this he was disappointed.

Sarah's idea was to kill Sylvester with good food, with kindness in a sense, with wifely *duty*. She was going to cook more and more elaborately. Sylvester already had a paunch, the doctor had cautioned him about overeating, not enough exercise and all that rot, but Sarah knew enough about weight control to know that it was what you ate that counted, not how much exercise you took. And Sylvester loved to eat. The stage was set, she felt, and what had she to lose?

She began to use richer fats, goose fat, olive oil, and to make macaroni cheese, to butter sandwiches more thickly, to push milk-drinking as a splendid source of calcium for Sylvester's falling hair. He put on twenty pounds in three months. His tailor had to alter all his suits, then make new suits for him.

'Tennis, darling,' Sarah said with concern. 'What you need is a bit of exercise.' She was hoping he'd have a heart attack. He now weighed nearly sixteen stone, and he was not a tall man. He was already breathing hard at the slightest exertion.

Tennis didn't do it. Sylvester was wise enough, or heavy enough, just to stand there on the court and let the ball come to him, and if the ball didn't come to him, he wasn't going to run after it to hit it. So one warm Saturday, when Sarah had accompanied him to the courts as usual, she pretended to faint. She mumbled that she wanted to be taken to the car to go home. Sylvester struggled, panting, as Sarah was no lightweight herself. Unfortunately for Sarah's plans, two chaps came running from the club bar to give assistance, and Sarah was loaded easily into the Jag.

Once at home, with the front door closed, Sarah swooned again, and mumbled in a frantic but waning voice that she had to be taken upstairs to bed. It was their bed, a big double one, and two flights up. Sylvester heaved her into his arms, thinking that he did not present a romantic picture trudging up step by step, gasping and stumbling as he carried his beloved towards bed. At last he had to manoeuvre her on to one shoulder, and even then he fell on his own face upon reaching the landing on the second floor. Wheezing mightily, he rolled out from under her limp figure, and tried again, this time simply dragging her along the carpeted hall and into the bedroom. He was tempted to let her lie there until he got his own breath back (she wasn't stirring), but he could anticipate her recrimination if she woke up in the next seconds and found he had left her flat on the floor.

Sylvester bent to the task again, put all his will power into it, for certainly he had no physical strength left. His legs ached, his back was killing him, and it amazed him that he could get this burden (nearly eleven stone) on to the double bed. 'Whoosh-sh!' Sylvester said, and went reeling back, intending to collapse in an armchair, but the armchair had rollers and retreated several inches, causing him to land on the floor with a house-shaking thump. A terrible pain had struck his chest. He pressed a fist against his breast and bared his teeth in agony.

Sarah watched. She lay on the bed. She did nothing. She waited and waited. She almost fell asleep. Sylvester was moaning, calling for help. How lucky, Sarah thought, that Edmund was parked out with a baby-sitter this afternoon, instead of a baby-sitter being in the house. After some fifteen minutes, Sylvester was still. Sarah did fall asleep finally. When she got up, she found that Sylvester was quite dead and becoming cool. Then she telephoned the family doctor.

All went well for Sarah. People said that just weeks before, they'd been amazed at how *well* Sylvester looked, rosy cheeks and all that. Sarah got a tidy sum from the insurance company, her widow's pension, and gushes of sympathy from people who assured her she had given Sylvester the best of herself, had made a lovely home for him, had given him a son, had in short devoted herself utterly to him and made his somewhat short life as happy as a man's life could possibly have been. No one said, 'What a perfect murder!' which was Sarah's private opinion, and now she could chuckle over it. Now she could become the Merry Widow. By exacting small favours from her lovers – casually of course – it was going to be easy to live in even better style than when Sylvester had been alive. And she could still write 'Mrs' at the foot of letters.

The Female Novelist

She has total recall. It is all sex. She is on her
third marriage now, having dropped three chil-
dren on the way, but none by her present
husband. Her cry is: 'Listen to my past! It is more
important than my present. Let me tell you what
an absolute swine my last husband (or lover) was.'

Her past is like an undigested, perhaps indi-
gestible meal which sits upon her stomach. One
wishes she could simply vomit and forget it.

She writes reams about how many times she, or
her woman rival, jumped into bed with her husband. And how she paced the floor, sleepless –

virtuously denying herself the consolation of a drink – while her husband spent the night with the other woman, flagrantly, etc. and to hell with what friends and neighbours thought. Since the friends and neighbours were either incapable of thinking or were uninterested in the situation, it doesn't matter what they thought. One might say that this is the time for a novelist's invention, for creating thought and public opinion where there is none, but the female novelist doesn't bother inventing. It is all stark as a jock-strap.

After three women friends have seen and praised the manuscript, saying it is 'just like life', and the male and female characters' names have been changed four times, much to the detriment of the manuscript's appearance, and after one man friend (a prospective lover) has read the first page and returned the manuscript saying he has read it all and adores it – the manuscript goes off to a publisher. There is a quick, courteous rejection.

She begins to be more cautious, secures entrées via writer acquaintances, vague, hedged-about recommendations obtained at the expense of winy lunches and dinners.

Rejection after rejection, none the less.

'I *know* my story is important!' she says to her husband.

'So is the life of the mouse here, to him – or maybe her,' he replies. He is a patient man, but nearly at the end of his nerves with all this.

'What mouse?'

'I talk to a mouse nearly every morning when I'm in the bathtub. I think his or her problem is food. They're a pair. Either one or the other comes out of the hole – there's a hole in the corner of the bathroom – then I get them something from the refrigerator.'

'You're wandering. What's that got to do with my manuscript?'

'Just that mice are concerned with a more important subject – food. Not with whether your ex-husband was unfaithful to you, or whether you suffered from it, even in a setting as beautiful as Capri or Rapallo. Which gives me an idea.'

'What?' she asks, somewhat anxiously.

Her husband smiles for the first time in several months. He experiences a few seconds of peace. There is not the clicking of the typewriter in the house. His wife is actually looking at him, waiting to hear what he has to say. 'You figure that one out. You're the one with imagination. I won't be in for dinner.'

Then he leaves the flat, taking his address book and – optimistically – a pair of pyjamas and a toothbrush.

She goes and stares at the typewriter, thinking that perhaps here is another novel, just from this evening, and should she scrap the novel she had fussed over for so long and start this new one? Maybe tonight? Now? Who is he going to sleep with?

All stories in this collection from

LITTLE TALES OF MISOGYNY

'These little tales are tremendous fun – glorious hand
grenades lobbed at the reader by a gleeful, cackling
Patricia Highsmith' Dan Rhodes

'Extraordinary stories . . . etched in acid and
unforgettable. Let the reader beware' *Financial Times*

The title says it all. Long out of print, this cult classic
resurfaces with a vengeance. From the man who makes
the mistake of asking his prospective father-in-law for
his daughter's hand in marriage, to Oona the alluring
cave woman, in these provocative, often hilarious,
sketches Highsmith turns our next-door neighbours into
sadistic psychopaths lying in wait among white picket
fences and manicured lawns.

'Splendidly repulsive' *Observer*

'Vicious black humour' *Guardian*

'For eliciting the menace that lurks in familiar
surroundings, there's no one like Patricia Highsmith'
Time

THE GLASS CELL

Patricia Highsmith

'*The Glass Cell* has lost little of its disturbing power . . . Highsmith was a genuine one-off and her books will haunt you' *Daily Telegraph*

'Highsmith is a giant of the genre. The original, the best, the gloriously twisted Queen of Suspense' Mark Billingham

Prison is no place for an innocent man. Philip Carter has spent six years in prison for a crime he didn't commit. On his release, his beautiful wife is waiting for him. He has never had any reason to doubt her. Nor their friend, Sullivan. Carter has never been suspicious, or violent. But prison can change a man.

'One closes most of her books with a feeling that the world is more dangerous than one had ever imagined' Julian Symons, *New York Times Book Review*

'To call Patricia Highsmith a thriller writer is true but not the whole truth: her books have stylistic texture, psychological depth, mesmeric readability' *Sunday Times*

THOSE WHO WALK AWAY

Patricia Highsmith

'Patricia Highsmith's novels are peerlessly disturbing . . .
bad dreams that keep us thrashing for the rest
of the night' *The New Yorker*

Who hasn't imagined killing his wife?
Sydney Bartleby has, compulsively, repeatedly,
plotting methods and forging alibis. He's a thriller
writer after all. He even knows how he would
dispose of her body. When Alicia goes missing,
Bartleby struggles to convince anybody of his
innocence, caught in a trap of his own making . . .

'Her novels, with their mysterious non sequiturs, weird
pairings and moments of stifled comedy, have an
unearthly sheen all their own . . . Highsmith was a
genuine one-off, and her books will haunt you'
Daily Telegraph

'By her hypnotic art Patricia Highsmith puts the
suspense story into a toweringly high place in
the hierarchy of fiction' *The Times*

PATRICIA HIGHSMITH

sphere